Barbara Steinitz • WHO CARES!

Note: Only blue and orange dogs in picture
books are allowed to eat chocolate bonbons.
Unfortunately, no other dogs should eat
chocolate. It's not good for them.

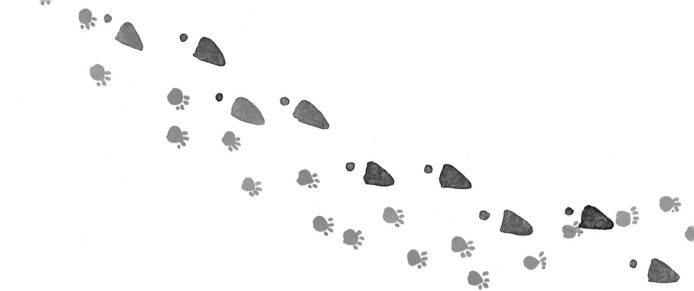

For Mom and Dad
. . . and Kocki, without whom
this story might never have
been told,

for Björn,

and especially
for Ingrid and Thomas.

 **STONE PAPER®**
Waterproof and tear resistant
Produced without water, without trees and without bleach
Saves 50% of energy compared to normal paper

WHO CARES!
Text and illustrations © 2009 Barbara Steinitz
This edition © 2018 Cuento de Luz SL
Calle Claveles, 10 | Urb. Monteclaro | Pozuelo de Alarcón | 28223 | Madrid | Spain
www.cuentodeluz.com
Published by agreeement with Von dem Knesebeck GmbH & Co. Verlag KG
Title in German: *Schnurzpiepegal*
First German edition published in 2009 by Bajazzo Verlag, Zurich
Second German edition published in 2018 by Von dem Knesebeck GmbH & Co. Verlag KG
English translation by Aisha Prigann
Printed in PRC by Shanghai Chenxi Printing Co., Ltd. July 2018, print number 1645-2
ISBN: 978-84-16733-34-7

WHO CARES!

Barbara Steinitz

Walking around the streets and parks
of most towns, you might notice that
many dogs look a lot like their owners.
Or perhaps it's the other way around:
do the owners all look
like their dogs?

Anton is cheeky and cheerful,
and so is his dachshund.

Some ladies have the same
long faces as their pekingese.

Ariela's poodle strides snootily through the world, just like she does.

Oskar is as fast and skinny as his greyhound.

The mysterious guy next door has the same hairdo as his puli.

People might think otherwise, but the neighbor's bull terrier is as mild-mannered as Mr. Luzi, who trained his dog really well.

But Leonora's dog . . .

. . . didn't look
anything like her.
Not one eensy-
weensy bit.

Leonora named her dog after her favorite opera, *Fidelio*. When she played the opera on her old gramophone, Fidelio sang along, and Leonora danced. The neighbors angrily banged broomsticks against the ceiling and shouted, "Make that dog stop howling!" But what do neighbors know about good music? Although, it has to be said, sometimes Fidelio also sang when the moon was out or the sun was shining or when it rained or when he was happy.

And when he was with Leonora, Fidelio was pretty much happy all the time.

But when Leonora took Fidelio for a walk, people would start to gossip. "Just look at that dog," they'd whisper, "He doesn't look anything like his owner! Incredible!"

They'd laugh at them,
but Leonora didn't mind.

Well, she did mind a **LITTLE** bit.

Two streets down lived Carmelo. And his dog . . .

. . . didn't look anything like him.
Not one eensy-weensy bit.

Carmelo loved making chocolate bonbons. He
often spent days coming up with original recipes
like marzipan fairy wings, violet truffles, pistachio
pebbles, pixie kisses with elderberry syrup,
crunchy kitty claws, nougat noodles . . .

Carmelo's dog was called Pistachia, because pistachio pebbles were her favorite, but really she liked all of his chocolate treats. After making bonbons, Carmelo wasn't always in the mood for chocolate. So Pistachia got lots and lots of bonbons . . .

When Pistachia didn't like a bonbon all that much, she'd growl softly. And when she really liked one, she'd wag her entire backside and roll around in a circle. They were very happy together.

But when Carmelo walked Pistachia, the gossipy whispers began. "Just look at that man! He doesn't look anything like his dog. Unbelievable!"

They'd turn up their noses and double over with laughter, but Carmelo didn't mind.

Well, he did mind a **LITTLE** bit.

And then, one day, it happened. Leonora's gramophone needle broke while she was playing her favorite record. She decided to walk Fidelio earlier than usual and buy a needle along the way. So she left the house at eight o'clock, not at ten like she normally did. If Leonora's gramophone needle hadn't broken, they might never have met: Leonora and Fidelio and Carmelo and Pistachia.

Leonora looked at Pistachia.
Carmelo looked at Fidelio.
There was nothing to say.
It was crystal clear.

They exchanged leashes and went home:
Leonora with Pistachia, and Carmelo with Fidelio.

After that nobody gossiped anymore.
Leonora and Carmelo could finally walk
their dogs in peace.

But something wasn't right.
Everything was the way it was supposed to be,
and yet Leonora felt a peculiar sadness that she
couldn't explain.

Pistachia wasn't happy either. It's not that
she didn't like opera. And Leonora always had
chocolate bonbons at home. Although they
where store-bought, they where quite delicious.
Pistachia didn't eat them though, and she didn't
roll around in circles anymore either.

Carmelo and Fidelio also felt out of sorts. It's not that Fidelio didn't like chocolate bonbons. All dogs like bonbons. And Carmelo even had a little radio. Of course, it didn't play Fidelio's favorite opera, but some other beautiful music. Fidelio didn't want to hear anything else, and he stopped singing.

So they got sadder and sadder: Leonora and Pistachia, Carmelo and Fidelio. And they couldn't figure out why. After all, everything was perfect now.

One day, Carmelo was listlessly working on a new bonbon creation when he accidentally burned the chocolate for the first time in his life. He had to scrub the burned pot for such a long time that he didn't walk Fidelio at eight o'clock, as he normally did, but at ten.

If Carmelo hadn't burned the chocolate, they might never have met a second time: Leonora and Pistachia and Carmelo and Fidelio.

Leonora looked at Carmelo.

Pistachia looked at Fidelio.

And Carmelo looked at Leonora.

And Fidelio looked at Pistachia.

Suddenly the strange sad feeling
was swept away.
There was nothing to say.
It was crystal clear.

And so, off they went . . .

Leonora and Carmelo.

Fidelio and Leonora.

Carmelo and Fidelio.

Pistachia and Fidelio.

Carmelo and Pistachia.

Leonora and Pistachia.

Now they do everything together: They listen to opera and sing and dance. They make chocolate bonbons and eat them all. They even roll around in happy circles.

People are very confused and say, "Those dogs aren't a good match, and the owners even less so. All together they look completely ridiculous!"

But the four of them don't mind.

Not even a **LITTLE** bit. They simply think . . .

. . . **WHO CARES!**